leapfrog

Rhyme Time

Goldilocks Rap

by Clare De Marco

Illustrated by Andy Rowland

W

FRANKLIN WATTS

C153869266

First published in 2009 by
Franklin Watts
338 Euston Road
London
NW1 3BH

Franklin Watts Australia
Level 17/207 Kent Street
Sydney
NSW 2000

A CIP catalogue record for this book is available
from the British Library.

ISBN 978 0 7496 9186 8 (hbk)
ISBN 978 0 7496 9192 9 (pbk)

Series Editor: Jackie Hamley
Editor: Melanie Palmer
Series Advisor: Dr Barrie Wade
Series Designer: Peter Scoulding

Printed in China

Franklin Watts is a division of
Hachette Children's Books,
an Hachette UK company.
www.hachette.co.uk

A girl called Goldilocks
with long, golden hair

went out for a walk in
the cool morning air.

A family of bears were
out walking, too.

Goldilocks found
their house.

6

What did she do?

She smelled something nice, so she walked inside.

She found three bowls of porridge laid out on the side.

As she tried the first bowl, her cheeks went red.

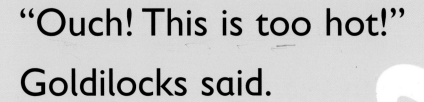

"Ouch! This is too hot!"
Goldilocks said.

Then she tried the
second bowl.
"Yuck! Too cold for me!

But what about the little
bowl that I can see."

"Yum, yum!" she said
and ate up the whole lot.

14

"That porridge was just right, not too cold, not too hot."

Goldilocks felt sleepy.

Three chairs she saw:

One too hard,

one too soft,

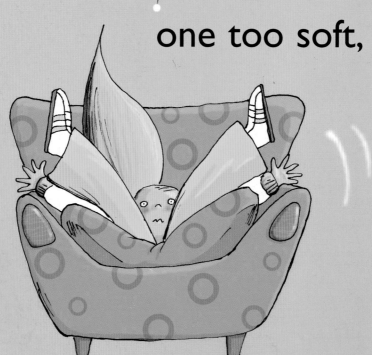

and one smashed
on the floor!

She climbed up the stairs
and found a big bed.

"Ouch, much too hard!"
she said, hitting her head.

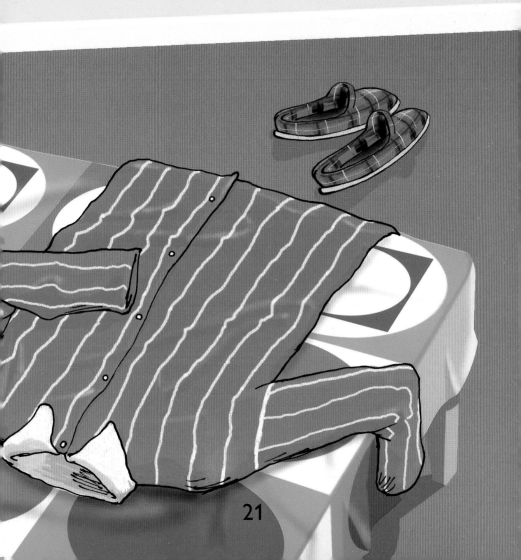

She tried the second bed.
"Much too soft for me!

But what about that little bed that I can see?"

She got into the little bed.
"It's just right!" she cried.

She fell fast asleep. Then
the door opened wide ...

A surprised Baby Bear
asked, "Who are you?"

"I'm Goldilocks,"
she stammered,
"It's nice to meet you."

27

She and Baby Bear were
friends for evermore.

Now she doesn't just walk in – she knocks on the door!

Puzzle 1

Put these pictures in the correct order.
Now retell the story in your own words.
Is there a lesson in the story?

Puzzle 2

hair	fair
share	gold

chair	tear
bear	rug

pot	spoon
forgot	hot

Find the non-rhyming word in each word box. Can you think of some words to rhyme with the odd one out?

Answers

Puzzle 1

The correct order is: 1f, 2b, 3e, 4d, 5a, 6c

Puzzle 2

The odd words out are:

gold, rug, spoon.

Look out for more Leapfrog Rhyme Time:

Mr Spotty's Potty
ISBN 978 0 7496 3813 3

Freddie's Fears
ISBN 978 0 7496 4382 9

Eight Enormous Elephants
ISBN 978 0 7496 4634 9

Squeaky Clean
ISBN 978 0 7496 6805 1

Felicity Floss: Tooth Fairy
ISBN 978 0 7496 6807 5

Captain Cool
ISBN 978 0 7496 6808 2

Monster Cake
ISBN 978 0 7496 6809 9

The Super Trolley Ride
ISBN 978 0 7496 6810 5

The Royal Jumble Sale
ISBN 978 0 7496 6811 2

But, Mum!
ISBN 978 0 7496 6812 9

Dan's Gran's Goat
ISBN 978 0 7496 6814 3

Lighthouse Mouse
ISBN 978 0 7496 6815 0

Big Bad Bart
ISBN 978 0 7496 6816 7

Ron's Race
ISBN 978 0 7496 6817 4

Boris the Spider
ISBN 978 0 7496 7791 6

Miss Polly's Seaside Brolly
ISBN 978 0 7496 7792 3

The Lonely Pirate
ISBN 978 0 7496 7793 0

Alfie the Sea Dog
ISBN 978 0 7496 7958 3

Red Riding Hood Rap
ISBN 978 0 7496 7959 0

Pets on Parade
ISBN 978 0 7496 7960 6

Let's Dance
ISBN 978 0 7496 7961 3

Benny and the Monster
ISBN 978 0 7496 7962 0

Bathtime Rap
ISBN 978 0 7496 7963 7

Woolly the Bully
ISBN 978 0 7496 7098 6*
ISBN 978 0 7496 7790 9

What a Frog!
ISBN 978 0 7496 7102 0*
ISBN 978 0 7496 7794 7

Juggling Joe
ISBN 978 0 7496 7103 7*
ISBN 978 0 7496 7795 4

I Wish!
ISBN 978 0 7496 7940 8*
ISBN 978 0 7496 7952 1

Raindrop Bill
ISBN 978 0 7496 7941 5*
ISBN 978 0 7496 7953 8

Sir Otto
ISBN 978 0 7496 7942 2*
ISBN 978 0 7496 7954 5

Queen Rosie
ISBN 978 0 7496 7943 9*
ISBN 978 0 7496 7955 2

Giraffe's Good Game
ISBN 978 0 7496 7944 6*
ISBN 978 0 7496 7956 9

Miss Lupin's Motorbike
ISBN 978 0 7496 7945 3*
ISBN 978 0 7496 7957 6

*hardback